Invitation to the Ball

Reader's Digest
Children's Books®

New York, New York • Montréal, Québec • Bath, United Kingdom

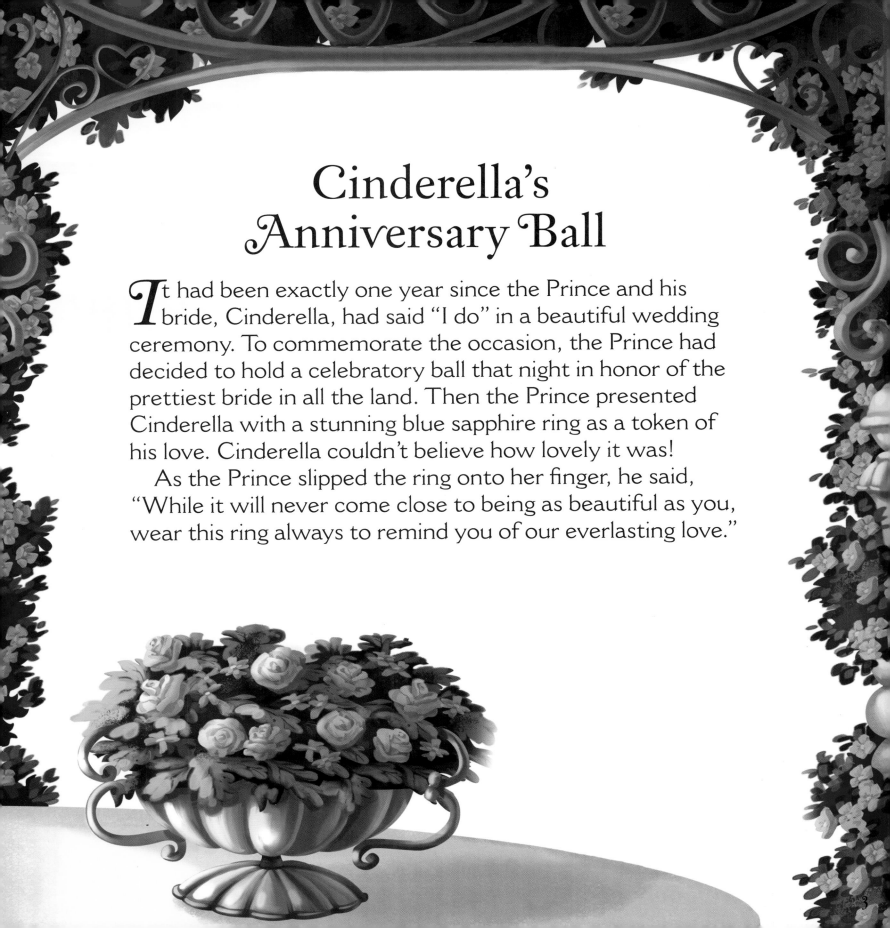

Cinderella's Anniversary Ball

*I*t had been exactly one year since the Prince and his bride, Cinderella, had said "I do" in a beautiful wedding ceremony. To commemorate the occasion, the Prince had decided to hold a celebratory ball that night in honor of the prettiest bride in all the land. Then the Prince presented Cinderella with a stunning blue sapphire ring as a token of his love. Cinderella couldn't believe how lovely it was!

As the Prince slipped the ring onto her finger, he said, "While it will never come close to being as beautiful as you, wear this ring always to remind you of our everlasting love."

Later that day, Cinderella removed her gloves to admire her sapphire ring once more, only to discover that it had slipped off her dainty finger!

"Oh, dear!" she cried. Cinderella looked in the pockets of her dress and turned her long white gloves inside out, but it was no use. The ring was gone!

"Don't worry, Cinderelly," said her mouse friend, Gus. "We'll help you find your ring."

Her little friend Jaq nodded. "Just leave it to us."

"All we have to do is retrace your steps," said Jaq.

"Why, that's a wonderful idea," Cinderella cried. "Now let's see. Just after the Prince gave me the ring, I ran up to my room to write about it in my journal."

"Let's go, Cinderelly!" Gus said excitedly as they all hurried to Cinderella's room.

"Is it there?" asked Jaq.

Cinderella shook her head sadly.

"Where did you go next?" Jaq asked.
Cinderella thought for a moment.
"Oh, yes. I went to the kitchen to make some tea!"

They all rushed to the kitchen, but the only ring they found there…was a sugar donut.

"Yum," said Gus, breaking off a piece. "Would you like a bite?"

Next, they went to the music room, where Cinderella had gone to practice a new song.

Cinderella and her mice friends thoroughly searched the entire area, but the only ring they left the room with…was the ringing in Jaq's ears!

"I read in the library for nearly an hour after that," Cinderella recalled.

But though they searched high and low, Cinderella's ring was nowhere to be found.

Cinderella glanced at the clock and began to grow a bit anxious. It would soon be time to dress for the ball! What if she couldn't find the ring in time?

"Don't worry," Jaq assured her. "We won't stop looking till we find your ring!"

Cinderella nodded. "I went to the stables to visit with Frou next," she said hopefully.

They hurried to the stables. While Jaq sifted
through piles of straw, Gus checked Frou's feed trough.
But Cinderella's sapphire ring simply wasn't there.

"The only other place I remember going," Cinderella said, "was to the garden to pick flowers for the ball."

The three of them rushed to the garden, but though Jaq and Gus found plenty of lovely, sweet-smelling flowers, they didn't find the princess's ring.

15

As they sadly walked back toward the palace, they passed the well. "Wait!" Cinderella cried. "I stopped at the well to draw some water for my flowers!"

"Maybe your ring fell into the well," Jaq declared.

"I don't think so," Gus said, trembling in fear.

"Come on," Jaq said, grabbing Gus's arm. "We're gonna find Cinderelly's ring. We promised!"

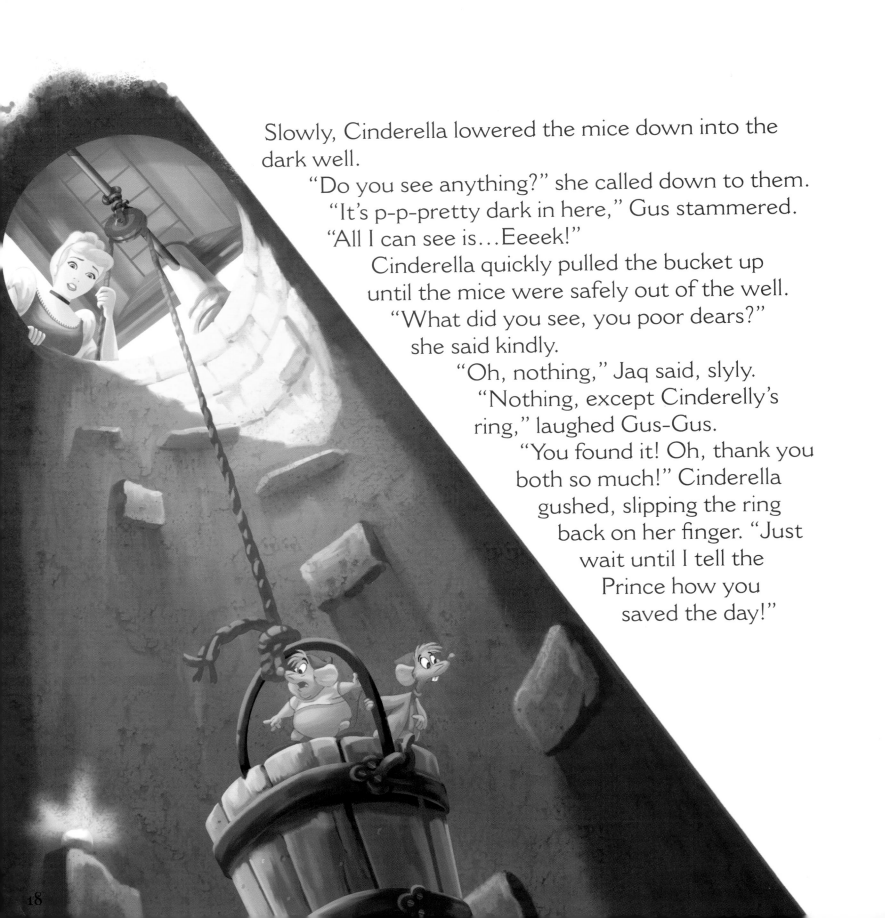

Slowly, Cinderella lowered the mice down into the dark well.

"Do you see anything?" she called down to them.

"It's p-p-pretty dark in here," Gus stammered. "All I can see is...Eeeek!"

Cinderella quickly pulled the bucket up until the mice were safely out of the well.

"What did you see, you poor dears?" she said kindly.

"Oh, nothing," Jaq said, slyly.

"Nothing, except Cinderelly's ring," laughed Gus-Gus.

"You found it! Oh, thank you both so much!" Cinderella gushed, slipping the ring back on her finger. "Just wait until I tell the Prince how you saved the day!"

That night, with the Prince by her side, and the "lost and found" sapphire ring safely on her finger, Cinderella declared Jaq and Gus her guests of honor. And as the couple danced the night away at their anniversary ball, they were reminded of how lucky and blessed they were to have found each other.

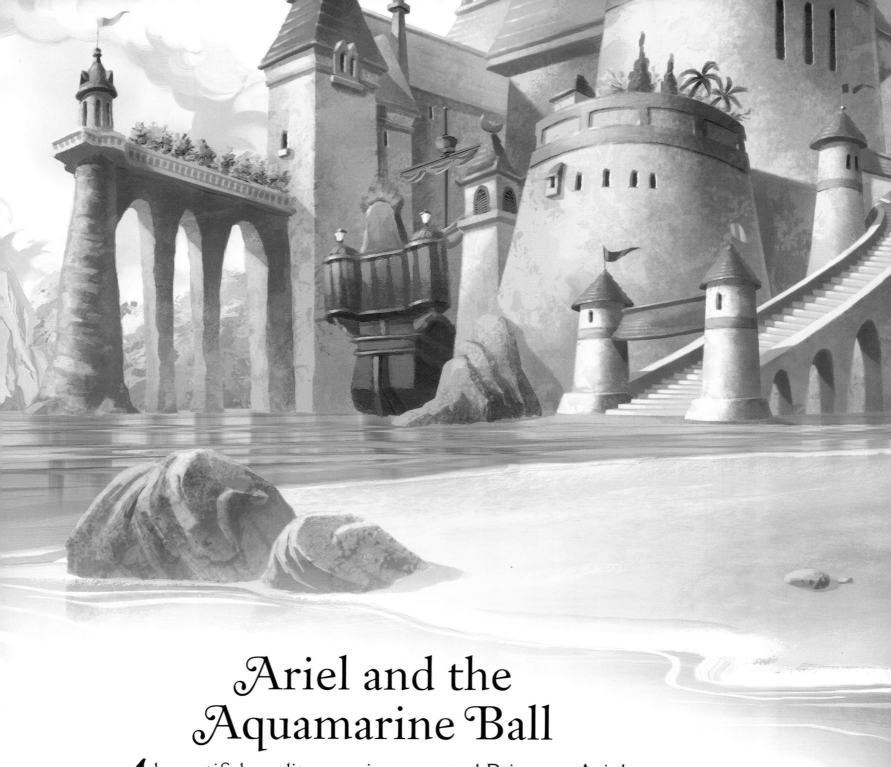

Ariel and the Aquamarine Ball

A beautiful sunlit morning greeted Princess Ariel as she set out for her daily walk along the sea. It was so lovely, in fact, that she decided to walk along the sandy shore farther than she ever had before.

Ariel's friend Scuttle, who had joined the
princess, suddenly let out a loud squawk!
"What is it, Scuttle?" Ariel asked.
Looking down, she spotted something
gleaming in the sand. She picked it up,
brushed the sand off, and then held
the object up in the sunlight to
get a closer look.

"Oh, I know what this is, Princess," declared Scuttle. "It's a piece of stickymabobber! It looks mighty tasty." And with that, he licked it! "Ick, ick, ick!" Scuttle coughed. "Or not."

Ariel giggled. "Do you mean 'candy'?" she asked.

"Well, I suppose some humans might call it that, yes," Scuttle said with a ruffle of his feathers.

"It does look just like candy, Scuttle," said Ariel kindly, "but it's actually a jewel."

And what a beautiful jewel it was. "But where did it come from?" Ariel wondered aloud. "I've never seen anything like it in the kingdom."

Scuttle shrugged. "It must've come from somewhere."

"What a lovely blue-green color it is, just like the sea," Ariel said, holding the jewel up to the sun. "That's it!" she cried. "It must be from the sea!" Ariel knew just what to do. "Scuttle, please go find Sebastian and ask him to get my father."

In no time, King Triton appeared in front of his daughter. "Ariel, how wonderful to see you," he said lovingly. "Is anything the matter?"

"No, Father," said Ariel, smiling. "It's just that I found this aquamarine jewel in the sand and I thought you might know who it belonged to."

27

King Triton looked astonished when he saw the jewel in his daughter's hand. "Yes, I know exactly who it belonged to," he said sadly.

"Please tell me," Ariel said.

"It will be far better if I show you," the king said. And with a blast of his trident, he transformed Ariel back into a mermaid.

Ariel dove into the sea and swam alongside her father all the way to Atlantica, loving the way it felt to swim through the water. It was as if she'd never left. But her pleasure soon faded when her father showed her to his throne room. Once magnificent, the room now looked as if it had been hit by a tidal wave.

"Atlantica's treasure!" Ariel cried. "What happened to it?"

King Triton shook his head. "A rogue wave," he said. "For hundreds of years, our kingdom's treasure was safe. And then suddenly, everything was washed away."

"Everything except the aquamarine jewel that I found on the shore," Ariel added sadly.

The king nodded. "We've been searching for the lost treasure ever since, but to no avail."

"Don't give up, Father!" Ariel cried. "I found the aquamarine necklace, didn't I? Now I'm going to help you find the rest of Atlantica's lost treasure!" And with a swish of her mermaid tail, she was gone.

Ariel's first stop was the old sunken ship—a place she remembered exploring as if it were yesterday. Darting in and out of the galleon, she soon managed to find nearly a dozen of the beautiful lost jewels.

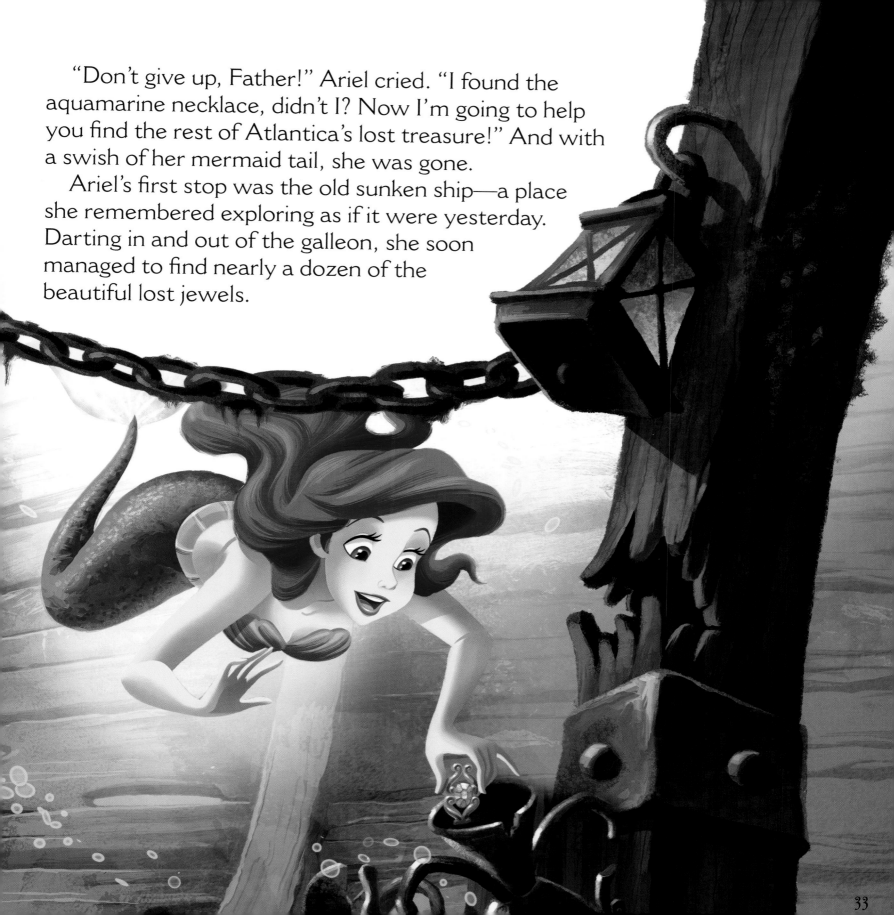

Then it was off to the coral reef, where,
with help from Flounder and some other friends,
she located even more of the missing jewels.

34

Ariel swam to every underwater place she could remember, and by the time the tide had come in, nearly all of Atlantica's lost treasure had been found.

King Triton had never been more proud. "Thanks to you, my dearest daughter," he said, "the kingdom's treasure is now back where it belongs."

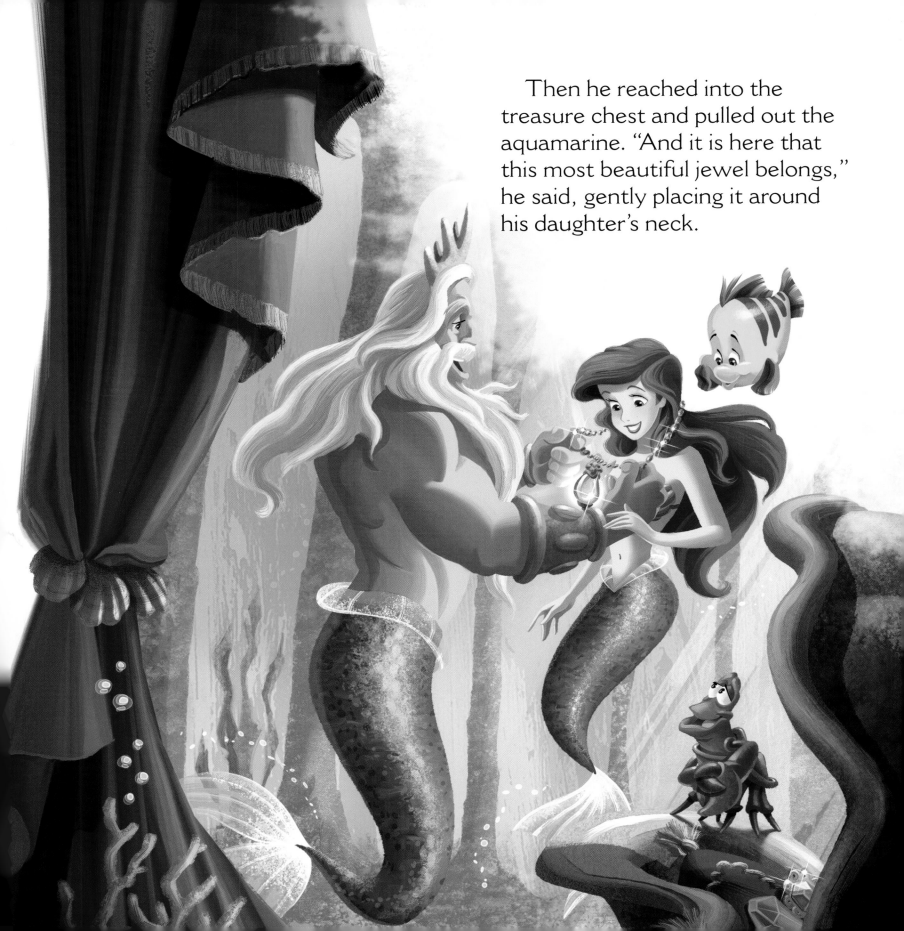

Then he reached into the treasure chest and pulled out the aquamarine. "And it is here that this most beautiful jewel belongs," he said, gently placing it around his daughter's neck.

Then, with both sadness and joy, the king said goodbye, turning Ariel into a human once again so she could return to the life she had chosen.

Eric rushed out to greet his wife as she ran up the steps of the palace. "Where have you been, my love?" he asked.

Ariel told Eric all about the adventure she'd had that day…about the aquamarine, the lost treasure, and how wonderful it was to see her father again and help Atlantica.

That evening, Prince Eric decided to hold a grand ball to celebrate not only the return of the lost jewels of Atlantica, but also the return of the most precious treasure of all…his beautiful wife, Princess Ariel.

Aurora's Birthday Ball

On the morning of her seventeenth birthday, Aurora opened her eyes to a beautiful sunny day. She smiled and stretched, excited to see what surprises this special day would bring.

She had just finished dressing for the day when her mother, the Queen, entered her room.

"Good morning, my darling," said the Queen. "Happy seventeenth birthday!"

"Oh, thank you!" Aurora said, turning to greet her mother. She quickly noticed that her mother had on a beautiful crown she'd never seen before. "What a lovely crown you're wearing, Mother!"

"Yes, it is lovely, isn't it?" the Queen said with a smile. "And soon it will belong to you."

"Come with me, my darling," the Queen said, leading her daughter to a great hall filled with royal portraits. One wall was filled with paintings of beautiful young princesses, each of them wearing a crown just like the one the Queen wore.

"Is that you, Mother?" Aurora asked, gazing up at the last portrait on the wall.

The Queen nodded. "It was painted on my birthday, right after my mother gave this crown to me. The tradition in our kingdom is that on a princess's seventeenth birthday, this crown is to be handed down to her by her mother."

"So you'll be passing that beautiful crown on to me today?" Aurora asked.

The Queen smiled. "I hope to, Aurora. But there's another part to the tradition. You see, you must first answer three riddles in order to 'earn' the crown."

"Oh, I love riddles!" Aurora exclaimed.

Just then, the three good fairies appeared. "Happy Birthday, Princess Aurora!" said the fairies in unison.

"They're here to give you your clues," the Queen explained. Then she kissed her daughter on the cheek. "Good luck, my dear."

Flora gave Aurora her first clue:

It can come in a great variety of colors.
It always smells sweet to the nose.
It's delicate, yet it can hurt you deeply.
What could it be, do you suppose?

The princess only had to think for a moment before she knew the answer. "It's a rose!" she said, rushing to the garden. There, she picked a lovely pink rose and placed it in her hair.

"The next clue is a bit more difficult," said Fauna.

One receives this on their wedding day.
It can be placed on the hand or the cheek.
Certain types of letters are sealed with it.
What is it of which we speak?

Aurora sat down by the fountain and gazed at her reflection while she thought. "One certainly receives gifts on their wedding day. But while a gift could be placed in your hand, it wouldn't be placed on your cheek."

"I know! It's a kiss!" Aurora cried happily, bending down to give each of the fairies a kiss on the cheek.

"Very good, Princess," said Fauna, blushing ever so slightly.

"And now I have
the final clue for you,"
Merryweather declared.

*What is invisible but can
truly be felt?*
*What is so strong that
your heart it can melt?*
*What can you fall into
but not want to get out?*
*What is it that this last
clue could be about?*

Aurora was pondering
Merryweather's riddle when Prince
Phillip walked up leading Samson.
    "Aurora, my love!" he said with
a smile. "Happy birthday!"
    The moment she laid eyes on Phillip,
the answer to the final riddle came to her.

"I solved the three riddles, Mother!" Aurora cried,
rushing into the Queen's sewing room. She took the rose
from her hair and handed it to her mother, then gave her a
gentle kiss on the cheek.

"Well done, my darling daughter," the Queen exclaimed.
"But what about the answer to the final riddle?"

Happily, Aurora looked back at Prince Phillip. "Love,"
she said sweetly. "Love is the answer."

With pride, Aurora's mother removed the crown she wore and placed it gently on Aurora's head.

And a short while later, the
Princess posed for her royal portrait.

That night, a celebratory ball was held in honor of Aurora's seventeenth birthday. And as Prince Phillip led the beautiful Princess onto the dance floor, she couldn't believe what a wonderful birthday it had been. Not only had she found the answers to all the riddles, but she had found true love.

How to Use the Disney Princess
You're Invited Playset

Help Cinderella, Ariel, and Aurora decorate for the royal ballroom celebrations. Then help each of the princesses select the ball gowns and accessories that will turn the celebratory ball into a night to remember.

1. To set up the playset, empty the contents of the box and fold down the backboard to create the royal ballroom. Use the side doors as part of the scenery.

2. Choose the side of the scene card you would like to use as your background for play and place it inside the box.

3. Press out the princesses from the press-out sheets and attach them to the base.

4. Decorate the scene card using the sticker sheets.

5. Make the royal ballroom celebrations come to life with your imaginative play.